This igloo book belongs to:

EMILY CLARK

....

igloobooks

Published in 2013
by Igloo Books Ltd
Cottage Farm
Sywell
NN6 0BJ
www.igloobooks.com

FIR003 0613
2 4 6 8 10 9 7 5 3 1
ISBN 978-1-78197-475-9

Illustrated by Michael Garton

Printed and manufactured in China

Tiny Tales with Big endings

Caterpillar

igloobooks

Up in the rustling branches of Appleblossom Wood,
a small, yellow something was wobbling on a leaf.

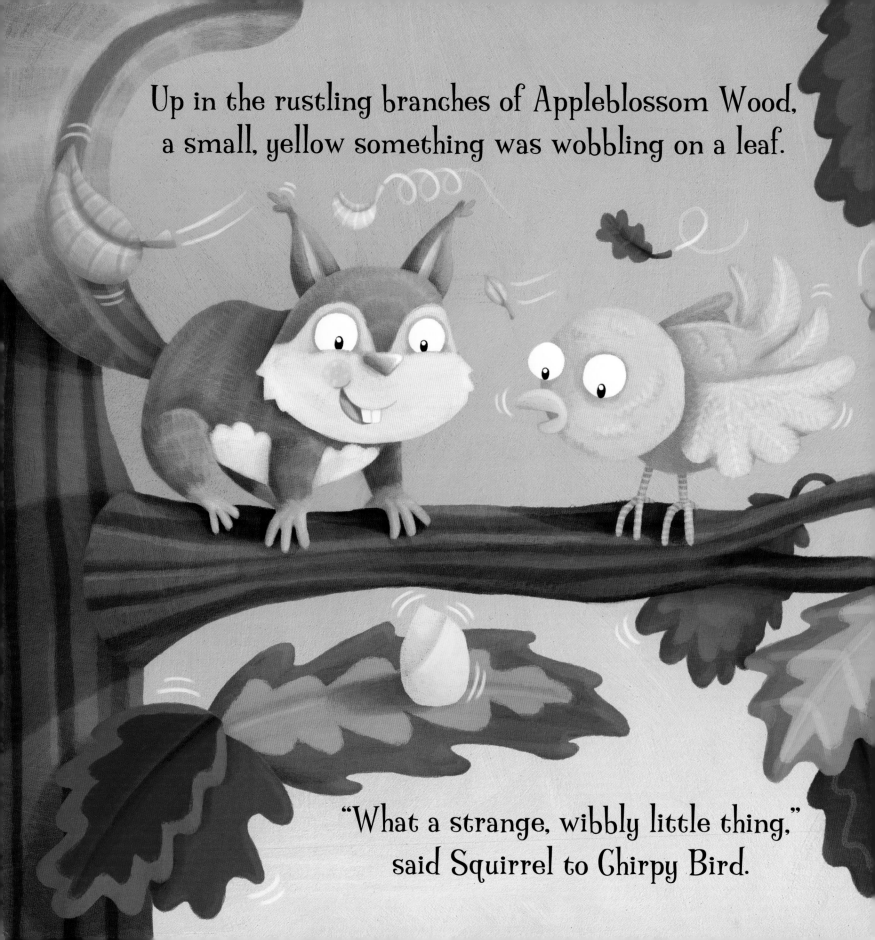

"What a strange, wibbly little thing,"
said Squirrel to Chirpy Bird.

A pair of twitchy feelers popped out,
followed by a wiggly, green body. "Oh my!"
cheeped Chirpy Bird. "A caterpillar."

Wiggly Caterpillar soon found the biggest, juiciest leaf in the wood and – CRUNCH! – munched a gigantic hole in it.

"Why are you so hungry?" buzzed Honey Bee.

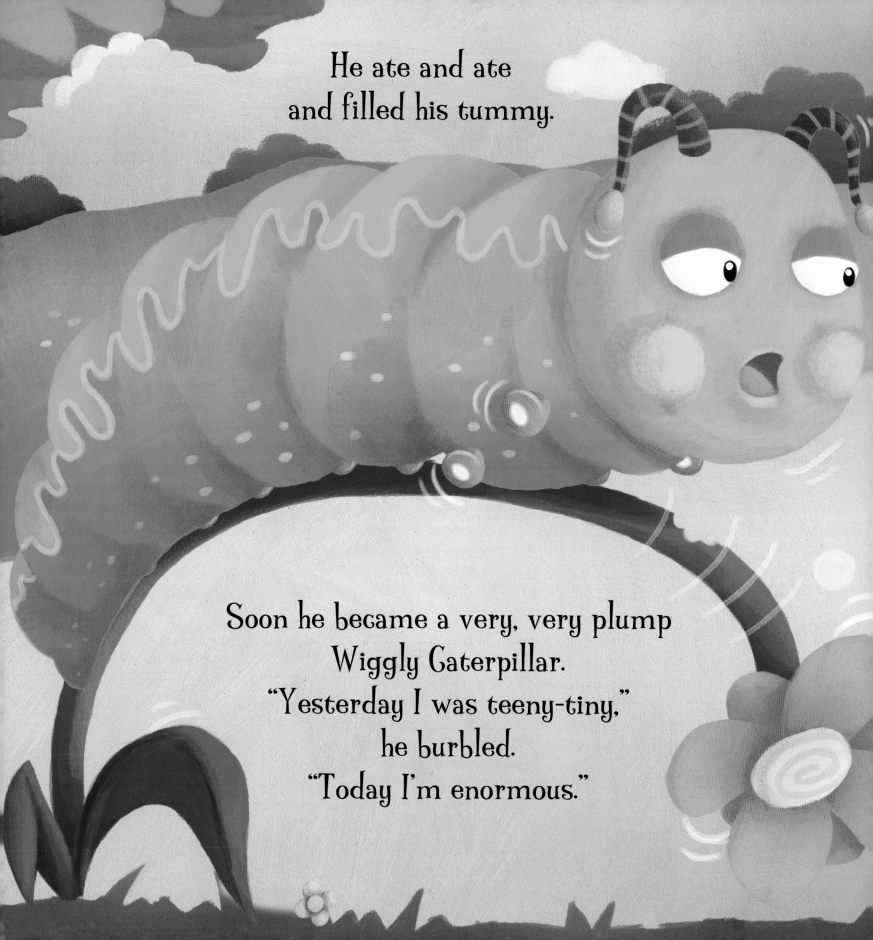

He ate and ate
and filled his tummy.

Soon he became a very, very plump
Wiggly Caterpillar.
"Yesterday I was teeny-tiny,"
he burbled.
"Today I'm enormous."

Wiggly Caterpillar suddenly became very tired.

"Why are you sleepy?" croaked Hoppity Frog.
"I don't know," yawned Wiggly Caterpillar,
"I must get some rest."

He spun a special, silvery bed
around himself, called a cocoon.
Once he was snug, Wiggly
Caterpillar fell fast asleep.

The animals all
watched quietly.
"What happens now?"
they whispered.

Wiggly Caterpillar slept for a long time.
One day, his cocoon began to crack open and with
a wonderful burst of rainbow colors, out wiggled...

... a butterfly!
"Hurray!" cheered the animals.

"Look at me!" Wiggly Butterfly giggled.
"Now I'm as beautiful as can be."

Tiny Tales with Big endings

Tadpole

There was something peculiar lying at the bottom of the pond on Honeyglade Farm.

"What could it be?" quacked Duc as he looked at it in wonder.

It looked like a bunch of jelly eggs, all huddled together, each with a little dot in the middle.

"Some of them have wiggly tails, too!" squeaked Mouse, excitedly.

A few weeks later, Ladybug saw something
moving underneath a lily pad.
"Hello," a voice burbled from the pond water.

"A little tadpole." said Ladybug.
"What happened to you?"

"I don't know," gurgled Little Tadpole,
"but I'm swimming free from my jelly egg and I've
got gills down my side that let me breathe underwater."

Little Tadpole soon became hungry and – CHOMP
– started to gobble up the juicy pond weed.
He munched and munched until,
one day, he began to change.

"Where has your tail gone?"
asked Rainbow Fish.

"I don't know," frowned Little Tadpole,
"but my gills are disappearing and
I've grown some legs, too!"

A few days later, Little Tadpole didn't look much like a tadpole at all.

His gills were gone, he had four legs and he could breathe through his mouth.

've got webbed feet, too," he giggled, happily.
The animals all began to smile.

"We've worked it out,"
they cheered.
"You've turned into..."

"... a frog!"

"What a wonderful surprise,"
croaked Little Frog.

"I'm so happy to
be grown up at last."